ALISON PRINCE

With illustrations by
Kevin Hopgood

Barrington Stoke

To the Lamlash Cubs, with love. Write on!

Visit Alison Prince's website:
www.alisonprince.co.uk

With special thanks to:
Amber Claybrook
Jade Claybrook
Harry Cook
Clarence Cudilan
Jack Eagle
Elliot Fane
Chloe Gilding
Sophie Hall
Chloe Hodges
Courtney Hutton
Barnaby Ogilvie
Scott Soanes

First published in 2010 in Great Britain by
Barrington Stoke Ltd
18 Walker Street, Edinburgh, EH3 7LP

www.barringtonstoke.co.uk

This edition first published 2013

ISBN: 978-1-78112-377-5

Printed in Great Britain by Charlesworth Press

Contents

Chapter 1
Football and Spiders

My name is Tim and I like football and spiders.
I like the way spiders spin their webs. I like it
when a spider runs over my hand. It feels nice.

Mum hates spiders. When I was younger, I took a spider to show her, but she screamed and jumped on a chair. The spider fell on the floor, and Dad stamped on it with his big feet. I was so upset that I hit Dad. Mum told me off and sent me to my room.

I have a spider in my room now. She's called Nancy. She spins big webs on my window. When a fly gets in her web, Nancy runs out to trap it. I spend ages watching her.

I used to keep Nancy a secret. If Mum and Dad asked what I was doing in my room, I'd lie and tell them, "Homework."

I used to hate homework. I hated French homework most of all, but then Max helped me. I kept him a secret too. In the end, I was trapped in a web with Max.

Chapter 2
The Perfect Plan

I play in goal for our football team. We train every Saturday morning. Mr Jarvis was our coach before Max. But then he got ill and had to stop. Max was a good coach. Max wasn't as old as Mr Jarvis, and he told us jokes.

Max told us a spider joke once. He said, "How can you tell when a football team is really bad?"

We didn't know.

"When there are spider webs across the other team's goal mouth," Max said.

We all got the joke and laughed. But my mate Kev didn't. He didn't get the joke.

I said, "Spiders take a long time to spin their webs. So it must be ages since the bad team scored a goal, because the ball would have ripped the spider webs."

"Oh, right," Kev said. But I don't think he got the joke even then.

I made a face. Max grinned at me behind Kev's back so Kev didn't see.

After training Kev told me that Max got the sack from his job in a café, but I didn't believe him. "Max is OK," I said.

In the changing room, Max said, "You're smart, Tim. You got my spider web joke."

I said, "I'm not smart. I can't do French."

"My mum used to work in France, so her French is great," Max said.

"My French is rubbish," I said. "I'm even worse than Kev. I can't do the homework. Dad got me a laptop and showed me a site called 'French Is Fun'. But it's no help."

The other kids had gone home by now. It was just Max and me in the changing room.

Max said, "I can help you if you like."

"Can you?" I said.

"When do you do your homework?" Max asked.

"On Sunday," I replied.

"OK," said Max. "Next week, hang around after football training and give me your homework. Is it questions, or do they want you to write stuff?"

"Questions," I said. "Like, fill in the missing words."

"Brill," said Max. "That makes it easy. I'll e-mail you the answers on Saturday night. On Sunday, all you have to do is copy them out. Then delete my e-mail."

"Wow!" I said. "Thank you!"

"No probs," said Max. "But it's our secret,
OK? You keep the secret, you get the answers.
You tell anyone, I stop." He wasn't smiling now.
"And then you'll be sorry."

I said, "I won't tell anyone. Promise."

I didn't tell anyone. Max e-mailed me the answers to my French homework, then I copied them out. Then I deleted his e-mail, like he said. Sometimes I made a mistake on purpose

so I didn't look too clever. But most of the time

that was OK. I started to get good marks.

Mrs Lee was our French teacher. "That's

better, Tim," she said. "Good work."

"Well done, Tim," Dad said. "I'm glad the

laptop is a help."

"It helps a lot," I told him.

But I didn't say how it helped. I didn't tell

Dad about Max and the e-mails.

Chapter 3
Don't Tell Anyone

After football on Saturday, I gave Max my homework, like I did every week. Mrs Lee had left to have a baby, so we had a new French teacher called Miss Potter.

But that Saturday, Max said, "Bit of a problem, Tim."

I was scared he was going to stop helping
me. "I haven't told anyone about the e-mails,"
I said.

"I know you haven't," said Max. "But helping
you takes a lot of my time. And time is money.
Is your homework worth a bit of money?"

My face went red. "Yes," I said.

"Pound a week?" Max asked.

I nodded.

"Starting now," Max said.

I had a pound coin in my pocket. Mum had given it to me to get some crisps on the way home. I gave it to Max.

"Thanks," he said. "This is secret too, OK? No messing me about or you'll be sorry."

"OK," I said.

The next day, I said, "Dad – can I have a bit more pocket money?"

"Sorry, Tim," Dad said. "Things are not too good just now."

He went back to his newspaper.

I went into the kitchen.

"Don't bother your dad," Mum said. "He's having a bad time. It looks like he may lose his job."

"Sorry," I said. I felt bad for asking.

"It's OK," Mum said. "You didn't know."

I went up to my room.

Nancy was in her web. She had trapped a fly and tied it up.

Chapter 4
Trapped

After a few weeks, Max said, "I need more money. It's £2 from now on, Tim. Sorry."

I didn't have £2. I gave him all the money in my pocket. £1.17. It was all I had. "I'll pay you the rest next week," I said.

"Don't forget," Max said.

I paid Max £2 a week when I could, but
sometimes I didn't have that much. Max said
he was keeping a record of what I owed him.

Then my dad lost his job. He kept trying to get a new one, but times were hard. There were no jobs.

Two Saturdays later, Max said, "My fee has gone up. It's £3 from now on."

"I can't get that much," I said.

"Do your own French homework then," Max said.

"I can't," I said. "You know I can't. Please don't stop helping me. Please!"

"It's up to you," Max said. "No money, no help."

I gave him £2.16. It was all I had.

Max put the money in his pocket and walked off.

Mum gave me dinner money so I could buy a burger or some chips. All my mates went out to the chippie. They didn't like school dinner.

They said it was all salad and stuff. For weeks I didn't buy chips. That way I had money for Max.

But one Saturday I only had £1.78 to give Max. It was all the money I had.

Max looked at it. Then he said, "OK, I'll do your homework this week. But my fee has been short for weeks. I charge more if you pay late. So now you owe me £15. And I want at least £5 next week."

I was starting to feel very scared of Max.

Then it was Saturday again. I didn't buy anything for dinner the day before, but I still didn't have £5 for Max. I only had £2.07.

"I told you £5," Max said.

"I'm sorry," I said. "I'll try harder next week."

"You'd better," Max said. "I want my money or else."

I kept thinking of what he'd said at the start. *You tell anyone, I stop. And you'll be sorry.*

I couldn't tell anyone.

I almost did something bad that day. Mum was out in the garden, hanging up the washing. Her purse was in her handbag.

I picked it up. I opened it. I was going to take some money – but I heard her come to the back door. I dropped the purse in her bag and ran to sit in front of the TV.

She came to find me. "Hi, love," she said. "You OK?"

"Fine," I said.

But I was scared that I might cry and then my mum would know something was wrong. So I ran upstairs. I felt trapped.

I put my finger on Nancy's web, very gently, but when I took my hand away the web had stuck to my finger and I'd torn a hole in it. Nancy rushed out and looked at the hole.

"I'm sorry," I said to Nancy. "I'm sorry."

And then I cried. But no one saw me.

Chapter 5
Alone with a Secret

Saturday came round again. I gave Max my homework questions and £2.44. It was all the money I had.

Max looked at the coins. Then he pushed me against the wall of the changing room. He put his face close to mine and said, "If that's the way you want it, OK. And don't forget, if you tell anyone, I'll know."

He hit the side of my head. "That's for starters," he said. Then he went out.

That Saturday, Max e-mailed me my homework, as usual. I didn't think he'd do it. I copied what he put in his e-mail. The French words I'd been given were really hard, so it was good he'd sent the answers. But I didn't know what I'd do the next week. I would have to get the money somehow. I'd have to tell Mum, but I couldn't, not when Dad had lost his job. I had to find a way to pay Max.

My spider had mended the hole I'd made in her web. I wished I was a spider. Spiders don't have to learn French. They don't need money. They spin their own webs and, if they get broken, they can mend them.

Chapter 6
Disaster

At school on Monday, Miss Potter said, "Tim. Come here."

She had my French homework on her desk.

"Is this your work?" she asked.

"Yes," I said.

"I see," said Miss Potter. "So you speak Spanish, do you?"

I smiled, in case it was a joke.

Miss Potter didn't smile. "This homework is not in French," she said. "It is in Spanish."

The other kids fell about laughing. I felt my face go red.

"I want to know what has been going on," Miss Potter said.

I didn't know what to say.

"Well?" said Miss Potter. "I'm waiting."

I had to tell her something, so I said, "I got my answers on the Internet."

Mrs Potter called my mum, and my mum came to the school. We sat outside the Head Teacher's room.

"You've let me down," Mum said. "You've let your dad down and yourself down. I don't know what to say to you."

The Head Teacher opened the door and said, "Come in."

She sat behind her desk. Mum and I sat on the other side.

"Well, Tim," Mrs Green said. "You've been cheating. That's not very clever, is it?"

I shook my head.

"You were using the Internet," said Mrs
Green. "Was it a blog of some sort?"

I didn't know what to say. I was like the
fly in Nancy's web. I'd never get out. I was
trapped for ever like the fly.

37

"So, tell me, Tim," Mrs Green went on. "Where did you find your answers?"

I shook my head. I was too scared of Max to say anything. His words were stuck in my mind. *You tell anyone, I'll know. You'll be sorry.*

"Tim, you have to tell us," Mum said.

"I can't," I said.

Mrs Green looked at my mum. "I think we have some sorting out to do," she said. "Leave it with me, and I'll come back to you." Then she said to me, "Tim, you can go home with your mum. I'll see you tomorrow."

"Thank you," Mum said.

I didn't say anything. Then Mum and I
went home.

Chapter 7
The Final Straw

"That's the final straw that is," Dad said. "I spend all day trying to get a job. I come home – and now this. Mum's told me everything, Tim. How do you think I feel?"

"I'm sorry," I said. I felt sick.

"What did you think you were doing?" Dad asked.

"I wanted to be – better," I said. I was trying not to cry.

"Don't worry, love," Mum said. "We'll sort it out."

But that's what I was scared of. I didn't want them to sort it out. Then they'd find out about Max and the money.

All the next week, the kids at school asked me, "What did you do? Why was your homework in Spanish?"

Kev didn't ask. Kev wasn't keen on school work, but his French had got much better too.

I kept thinking, 'On Saturday I will see Max.' I was still trying to find the money I owed him, but I knew it was no good.

On Saturday morning I was at home, not at football. "I don't want to go," I told Mum.

"But you love football training," Mum said.

I went up to my room. There was no sign of Nancy. Maybe she was dead like the fly.

Chapter 8
Good Mates

Then it was Monday again. I had to see Mrs Green, the Head Teacher, first thing.

"I have some news for you, Tim," she said. "The football team has a new coach. His name is Mr Gordon."

"Where has Max gone?" I said. "Is he coming back?"

"No," said Mrs Green. "Max has gone away."

Gone away! I shut my eyes. I felt dizzy.

"Now, about French," Mrs Green said. "We have a new French teaching assistant. Those of you who need extra help will work with her. She's very nice."

I didn't know what to say.

"You were not the only one, Tim," Mrs Green went on.

Not the only one. What did she mean?

"You deleted the e-mails, didn't you?" Mrs Green said. "As Max told you to do. But some boys did not."

I felt my face go red. She must have asked Mum and Dad to look in the deleted files on my laptop. So she knew. And Mum and Dad knew.

"Yes," said Mrs Green, as if I had spoken out loud. "We know what Max has been up to."

So that's why Max had gone. They had found out all about him. Then Mrs Green said, "Tim, listen. If you ever get scared again, you must tell someone. I know it's hard. You may have to admit that you did something silly. But it's better than being alone with a secret. Now, off you go, back to your class."

I went to the door. Then I said, "Thank you."

"That's OK," Mrs Green said. She smiled.

I didn't smile, but I felt a bit better.

At lunchtime, Kev and I went to the chippie. "What about Max, then?" Kev said.

"Gone," I said.

"I know," said Kev. He took a bite of his burger and wiped ketchup off his chin. "Max was helping me, too. And Mick and Tommy."

I nearly choked on my chips. "You're kidding," I said.

"He sent us all the same e-mails," said Kev. "But we didn't know. We kept it a secret."

"He told me to keep it a secret too," I said.
"So how did Max get found out?"

"I got fed up with him asking for so much
money," Kev said. "So, when he sent those
answers in Spanish, I told my brother Gary."

Gary works in a café after school. It's the same café where Max used to work.

"Gary sent all Max's e-mails to Mrs Green," said Kev. "I hadn't deleted them."

"Wow," I said. "So that's how she found out. Was she mad at you?"

"Yes, a bit," said Kev. "But she was much madder with Max. He was a rip-off and a thief. Know why he got the sack from the café?"

I shook my head.

"He was pinching money from the till," Kev said. "The man who owns the café didn't tell the police then, but he has now. That's why the cops came and got him." Kev finished his burger. "Buy you a Coke?" he asked.

"Thanks," I said. Kev was a good mate. He was too smart to find Max's jokes funny, not too stupid.

When I got home I saw that Nancy had laid eggs. They were in the corner of my window in a yellow cocoon spun out of web.

Mum came in when I was looking at the eggs. "Please don't scream," I said. "The spider is OK, Mum. It really is OK."

Mum took a deep breath, but she didn't scream. "Yes," she said. "Everything is OK."

And she hugged me and I knew that everything was OK.

Our books are tested
for children and young people by
children and young people.

Thanks to everyone who consulted on
a manuscript for their time and effort in
helping us to make our books better
for our readers.

*Also from **Barrington Stoke**...*

City Boy

Alan Combes

Josh loves football – but he needs to
get much better to play for City.

His grandad has a plan.

Can he help Josh get to play for his heroes?

United Here I Come!

Alan Combes

Jack and Jimmy are very bad at football.

But Jimmy is sure he will play for
United one day!

Is Jimmy crazy – or can he make it?

www.barringtonstoke.co.uk

*Also from **Barrington Stoke**...*

Help!

Alison Prince

Dad wants Ben's help.

He needs to fix a shower.

But what happens if Dad gets it wrong?

I Spy

Andrew Newbound

Finn borrows his spy dad's top secret work gear
to become 'School Spy'.

When Tom gets bullied, he calls on Finn to help
him out.

Can Finn and Tom beat the bullies together?

www.barringtonstoke.co.uk